Disney

Aladdin

KT-377-032

Ladybird

Once, in a faraway land,
deep in the desert, a dark man
waited on a dark night... with a
dark purpose...

Ladybird books are widely available, but in case of difficulty may be ordered by post or telephone from:
Ladybird Books – Cash Sales Department Littlegate Road Paignton Devon TQ3 3BE Telephone 0803 554761

A catalogue record for this book is available from the British Library

Published by Ladybird Books Ltd Loughborough Leicestershire UK
LADYBIRD and the device of a Ladybird are trademarks of Ladybird Books Ltd

The man's name was Jafar. He was the Sultan of Agrabah's most trusted adviser.

Jafar and his wicked parrot, Iago, watched impatiently over the starlit desert. Suddenly, they noticed a galloping horse churning up the sand and heading towards them. Its rider pulled up quickly in front of Jafar.

"You're late, Gazeem!" Jafar growled at the man.

"A thousand apologies, Great Jafar!" whined Gazeem, as he reached into his pocket. "But see – I have brought the missing half of the scarab medallion!"

At once Iago flew at Gazeem. He snatched the prized medallion and handed it to his master.

Jafar pulled out the matching half of the medallion from his robes and joined the two halves together. A perfect fit!

The scarab began to glow brightly.

BOOOM! A clap of thunder shattered the desert silence. The scarab sprang from Jafar's hand and sped away across the sand dunes.

"Quickly, follow the trail!" cried Jafar, spurring his horse into action. Gazeem mounted his own horse and raced along behind.

The horsemen chased the magic scarab far into the desert. At last it stopped abruptly and buried itself in a mound of sand and rock.

Jafar watched as the rock changed in front of him into the huge head of a Tiger-God. Its fierce jaws protected the entrance to a deep cave.

"Who disturbs my slumber?" roared the Tiger-God in fury.

"At last, Iago!" whispered Jafar. "After all my years of searching – the Cave of Wonders!"

"Awk!" screeched Iago. "Cave of Wonders!"

"Now remember," Jafar snarled at Gazeem. "Bring me the lamp. The rest of the treasure is yours, but the lamp is *mine*!"

Gazeem hesitated for a moment, then walked right inside the Tiger's mouth. Instantly, its gigantic jaws slammed shut upon the thief!

"Unworthy fool!" boomed the voice of the Tiger-God. "Only one may enter here. One whose rags hide a heart that is pure – the Diamond in the Rough!"

In the twinkling of an eye, the massive cave, its treasures, and Gazeem melted back into the desert.

"Awk! I can't believe this!" squawked the parrot. "Now we'll never get that stupid lamp!"

"Patience, Iago!" said Jafar. "Gazeem was obviously less than worthy."

"Now, *there's* a big surprise! So…"

Jafar squeezed Iago's beak tightly. "So… we must find the one who is!"

Late next morning, a ragged but kind-hearted boy, called Aladdin, stealthily watched the marketplace in Agrabah. Earlier he had stolen a loaf of bread from a stall and escaped onto a rooftop for safety. But today he and his monkey, Abu, would have no breakfast. For Aladdin had met two hungry children and given the stolen loaf to them.

Now Aladdin could see the Sultan's guards searching for him in the narrow streets below. He and Abu would have to remain hidden until the guards had gone. They sat down and tried to make themselves comfortable.

"Cheer up, Abu," said Aladdin, patting his friend's paw. "Some day it'll be better than this. Just you wait and see!"

Meanwhile, in the royal palace, time was running out for the Sultan's only daughter, Princess Jasmine.

"Dearest, you must stop rejecting every suitor," her father insisted. "The law says you must marry a prince by your next birthday. And there are only three more days left!"

"The law is wrong!" Jasmine exclaimed. "How can you force me to marry someone I do not love, Papa? Oh… I wish I'd never been born a princess!"

At this, the Sultan shuffled away to ask Jafar's advice.

"I'm sorry, Rajah," said Jasmine to her pet tiger.
"I can't stay here any longer. Tonight I'll disguise myself as a
servant, and escape from the palace. I'll miss you, Rajah!"

Inside the palace, the Sultan had explained the whole situation to his most trusted adviser.

"I may be able to find a solution to your problem," said Jafar, "but it will require the use of your Blue Diamond." Then he raised his magic cobra staff to the Sultan's eyes.

The Sultan was soon caught in a hypnotic trance. "Yes… of course!" he said to Jafar, giving him the ring.

Jafar hurried away into a secret passage and climbed a long flight of stairs to his tower laboratory. He clutched the Blue Diamond ring in his hand.

"Our moment draws near, Iago!" he said. "With this diamond, I can find…"

"Awk! A husband for Jasmine?" interrupted Iago.

"No, fool! The one who can get us the lamp!" said Jafar.

Early the next morning, Jasmine wandered in disguise through the city's bustling marketplace. Seeing a hungry little boy near a fruit stall, she picked up an apple and handed it to him.

"You'd better pay for that!" shouted the stall owner.

"Pay?" replied Jasmine, looking puzzled. She had never had to pay for anything before. "I'm sorry, sir, I haven't any money. But I'm sure I can get some from the Sultan."

"Thief!" bellowed the man, grabbing her by the arm. "Do you know what the penalty is for stealing?"

Suddenly a boy emerged from the crowd and stepped between the huge, angry man and the frightened girl. It was Aladdin! He quickly thought of a way to rescue her.

"Forgive my poor sister, oh merciful one!" he pleaded. "She didn't mean to steal! Sadly, she's a little crazy. She thinks my monkey is the Sultan. Now come along, Sis. Time to see the doctor."

Jasmine played along and bowed to Abu. Aladdin took her hand and led her away to the safety of the rooftops.

Back in the palace, Jafar's secret laboratory was ablaze with light.

"Show me the one who can enter the cave!" the evil sorcerer demanded. He placed the Blue Diamond ring in an enormous, magic hourglass.

The swirling sands of time parted, revealing the face of a boy on a rooftop in Agrabah. Jafar smiled menacingly and looked at Iago.

"Have the guards bring him to the palace!" he ordered.

The palace guards marched at once into the city and discovered where Aladdin and Jasmine were hiding. Before Aladdin could even leap to his feet, he was taken prisoner.

Jasmine threw back her hood and shouted angrily at the guards, "Unhand him, by order of the Princess!"

"The Princess?" gasped Aladdin in surprise.

"I'm sorry, Your Highness," the chief guard exclaimed, "but I dare not release him. My orders come from Jafar. You will have to take it up with him."

"Believe me, I will!" said Jasmine firmly, as the guards led Aladdin away.

In the cold, dark dungeons of the palace, Aladdin thought about the beautiful girl and knew that he had fallen in love with her.

"But she's a princess! I can't believe it!" he said aloud to Abu, who had followed him into the dungeon and unlocked his chains. "And I thought she was as poor as we are!"

"You don't have to be poor for ever," said a wizened old beggar behind him. "A cave filled with treasure can be yours if you will just help an old man to get a worthless old lamp!"

Abu's eyes lit up at the mention of treasure, but Aladdin hesitated. Then, thinking of Jasmine, he struck a deal with the beggar. Aladdin didn't know that it was Jafar in disguise.

The old man led the way through a secret passage, and they escaped into the desert. Soon the Cave of Wonders rose before Aladdin's eyes, and Jafar pushed him forward.

"Who disturbs my slumber?" thundered the Tiger-God.

"Uh... it is I... Aladdin!"

"Proceed," said the voice. "Touch nothing but the lamp!"

"Quickly, my boy," urged the old man. "Fetch me the lamp and you shall have your reward." Then he watched Aladdin and Abu disappear into the cave.

Aladdin and Abu walked deeper and deeper into the cave down a winding staircase, until they came to a huge chamber filled with golden treasure. They could not believe their eyes. Without thinking, Abu reached towards a glittering casket.

"No, Abu!" warned Aladdin. "We mustn't touch *anything* until we find the lamp. Come on. This way!"

Suddenly Abu noticed something following them. He could see a richly embroidered carpet peeping out from behind a pile of gold coins.

"A magic carpet!" cried Aladdin. "Come on out! We won't hurt you. Maybe you can help us to find the lamp."

Instantly the friendly carpet took off in excitement and pointed the way into a second chamber.

In the strong blue light Aladdin could see a huge staircase in the centre of a lake. Right at the top, a small object reflected a ray of light.

"It must be the lamp!" cried Aladdin, running towards it. But Abu had spotted a magnificent ruby in the hands of a statue. He grasped the jewel between his paws.

At once the ground started to tremble and the Tiger-God spoke again.

"You have touched the forbidden treasures! Now you will never again see the light of day!"

Aladdin snatched the lamp just as the staircase started to crumble beneath him. He lost his balance and began to fall towards the lake, which had turned to boiling lava. Fortunately, he was caught in time by the magic carpet. They hurried to rescue Abu from danger and sped towards the entrance. The cave walls collapsed noisily behind them.

"Help us!" shouted Aladdin as soon as he saw the beggar.

"The lamp! Give me the lamp!" cried the old man excitedly. And he seized it from Aladdin's hand. Then Jafar pulled a long dagger from his robes and bent down to strike Aladdin.

"Goodbye, fool!" snarled Jafar.

In a flash, Abu sank his teeth into the chief adviser's arm.

Jafar howled in pain and dropped the dagger. Suddenly the whole cave gave way and Aladdin and Abu were swallowed up inside.

The earthquake had stopped and everywhere was silent. Aladdin opened his eyes. The treasure had disappeared.

"We're trapped in here, Abu!" he despaired. "That jackal stole the lamp! Now he'll never come back for us!"

Abu chirped and danced around, holding up his paws. Then Aladdin's eyes widened. The little thief was holding the lamp!

"Good work, Abu!" he said, taking the lamp. "But what's so special about this dusty old thing, anyway?" wondered Aladdin, rubbing off the dirt. At once, the lamp started to glow.

A towering cloud of smoke poured from the spout and formed itself into a gigantic figure! Chattering away as it changed its shape, the giant at last looked down at Aladdin.

"I am the Genie direct from the lamp," said the amazing creature. "I can grant you three wishes. But listen, here are the rules. One, I can't kill anybody. So don't ask. Two, I can't make anyone fall in love with anybody else. Three, I can't bring anyone back from the dead. So, what's your first wish, Aladdin?"

Aladdin liked the Genie and decided to tease him. "I'm not sure!" he said. "If you were a *real* genie, you would have got us out of this cave by now!"

Quick as a wink they were soaring through the air on the magic carpet. Soon they landed on a desert oasis.

"How's that, Aladdin? Am I a genie, or am I a genie?"

"I guess you're a genie, all right!" said Aladdin. "So, do I get my three wishes?"

"Yep!" said the Genie. "But no more freebies and no fair wishing for three more wishes!"

Aladdin thought at once of Princess Jasmine. "I wish…" he said, "I wish to be a prince!"

Meanwhile, at the palace, Jafar came face to face with a very angry princess.

"I command you to release the boy arrested in the market," she ordered.

"But he has already been… executed," lied Jafar. "I am sorry, Your Highness."

"When I marry and become Queen, you'll pay for this, Jafar!" cried Jasmine, fighting back her tears. She turned and walked away.

"Iago, that girl means trouble!" said Jafar. "Her wedding march will be our funeral march!"

"Not if you marry her yourself!" Iago suggested.

"Excellent! I love the way your foul little mind works," said Jafar.

At that very moment, an unexpected visitor arrived.

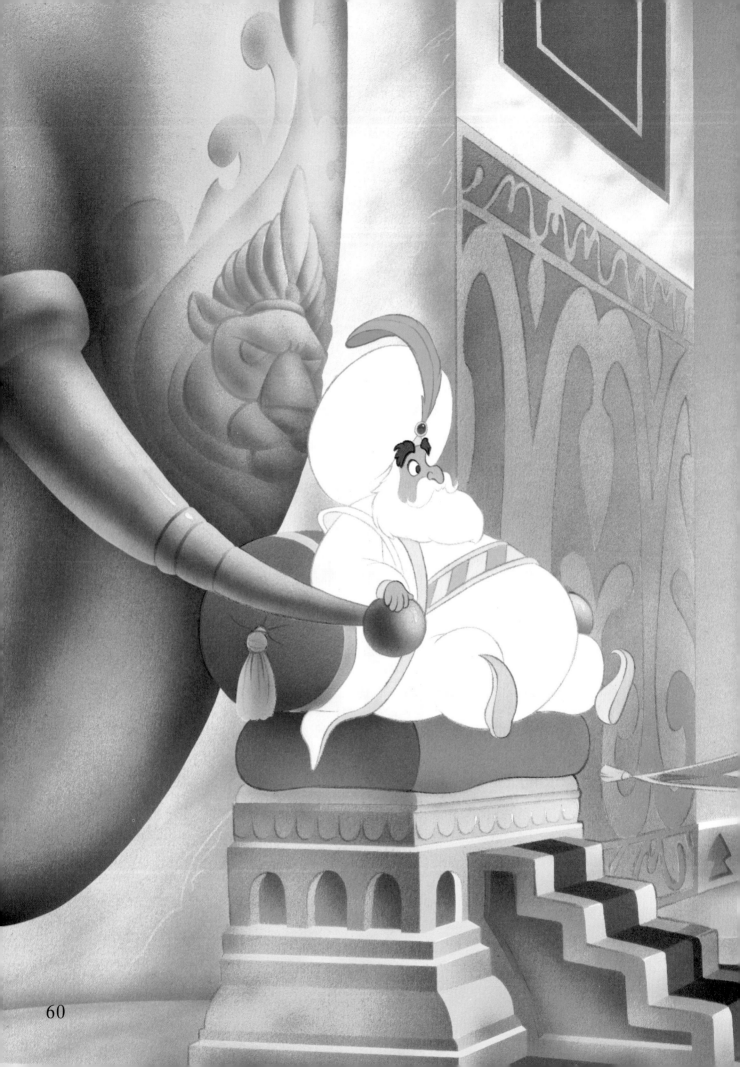

The palace gates were thrown open to make way for a magnificent procession.

"Prince Ali Ababwa!" announced a palace guard. Trumpets blared! Drums rolled! And into the throne room flew Aladdin on his magic carpet!

He was dressed from turban to toe in the silks and jewels of a royal prince!

"I have come to seek the hand of the Princess Jasmine," he said to the astonished Sultan.

That night Prince Ali took the Princess for a moonlit ride over the city on the magic carpet. Jasmine recognized his voice and asked if he was the boy she had met in the market. But Aladdin felt that he could not tell her the truth, and pretended he really *was* a prince.

By the time the carpet had returned to the palace balcony, Jasmine knew that this was the Prince she wanted to marry.

But Jafar had other plans. Aladdin glided happily down to the ground on the magic carpet... and fell right into the hands of the palace guards.

Bound and gagged, Aladdin was carried to the edge of a high cliff. He could hear angry waves crashing down below.

"So you like to fly, Prince Ali?" said one of the guards. "Well, try this!" And they threw Aladdin over the side, into the swirling sea!

Aladdin dropped like a stone. But as he sank deeper, the lamp fell from his turban. He strained against the ropes, until one hand was free, and managed to touch the lamp.

At once the Genie appeared. "Never fails!" he complained. "You get in the bath, and there's a rub at the lamp…" Then he realized Aladdin was drowning. "I guess you wish I'd get you out of this mess!"

Aladdin's head bobbed in the water. "I'll take that as a 'Yes'," added the Genie.

Once Prince Ali was out of the way, Jafar told Jasmine to go to the throne room. "Your father has something to tell you, Princess," he smirked.

"You will… marry… Jafar!" droned the hypnotized Sultan when she entered the room.

"Never! I've *chosen* Prince Ali," cried Jasmine. "Papa! What's wrong with you?"

"I know!" said a familiar voice from the doorway.

It was Prince Ali. "This traitor has been hypnotizing you, Your Majesty!" he said, snatching the cobra staff from Jafar and smashing it against the ground.

Jafar fled for his life – but not before he had glimpsed the lamp in the Prince's turban.

"So Prince Ali is no more than that ragged street urchin, Aladdin!" Jafar told Iago in the safety of his laboratory. "*And* he has the lamp! Now, listen carefully to my plan."

At dawn the next morning, Iago flew silently into Aladdin's room, stole the lamp and took it to Jafar.

"At last!" said Jafar. He eagerly rubbed the lamp and watched the Genie appear.

"I am your master now," declared Jafar.

"I was afraid of that," said the Genie.

"Keep quiet, slave!" snapped his new master. "Grant me my first wish. I wish to be the Sultan."

That day, nearly everyone in Agrabah came to the palace and crowded beneath the balcony to hear the Sultan's happy news.

"My daughter has chosen Prince Ali to be her husband!" the Sultan announced to the cheering throng.

But suddenly the sky darkened and everyone fell silent. A tall, dark figure came to the front of the balcony.

"Now, you miserable wretches, you will bow to *me*," said Jafar.

"We will *never* bow to you!" said Jasmine angrily.

"Then you will cower!" exclaimed Jafar, rubbing the lamp again. "Slave, my second wish is to be the most powerful sorcerer in the world!"

"I don't like it, but you've got it, Master!" the Genie replied.

"And for my first trick, I will banish Aladdin to the ends of the earth!" continued the sorcerer.

Bolts of lightning snapped from Jafar's fingertips, hurling
Aladdin, Abu and the magic carpet far away to a snowy
mountain top. Aladdin and his friends realized they had to
escape from this dangerous place or they would freeze to death.

"I must get back and set things straight," said Aladdin.
He turned and saw the carpet pointing the way to Agrabah.

Meanwhile, Jafar had taken command of the palace. Jasmine was now his servant, and her father had been turned into a puppet, hanging from the ceiling.

"Genie," said Jafar, "my final wish is for Princess Jasmine to fall deeply in love with me."

"But Master," said the Genie, "I can't do that…"

Jafar shook with anger at the Genie's answer. Then suddenly he saw a flash of steel. He couldn't believe his eyes.

"*You!*" he snarled, conjuring up a wall of fire. "How many times do I have to get rid of you, boy?"

Aladdin jumped over the flames. "Are you afraid to fight me, you cowardly snake?" he challenged.

"A snake, am I?" Jafar replied. "So be it!"

Jafar became a huge cobra and raised his head to strike. "So, you thought you could outwit the most powerful being on earth," he said, hissing loudly.

Aladdin's mind worked quickly. "The Genie has more power than you'll ever have, Jafar!" he cried.

"You're right!" agreed the power-mad Jafar. He caught the lamp in his coils.

"Slave, my third wish is to be an all-powerful genie!"

"Your wish is my command!" said the Genie in disbelief.

The cobra vanished, and Jafar towered over everyone in the shape of a genie. "Now I have absolute power!" he crowed.

But before Jafar could say another word, gold chains clasped his wrists and he was sucked with Iago into a lamp that had magically appeared.

Instantly the palace returned to normal. Aladdin looked at the Princess. "I'm sorry I lied to you. I do love you, but I cannot go on pretending to be a prince when I'm really just a poor street boy."

Then he turned to the Genie. "Genie, with my final wish I give you your freedom… but I'll miss you."

Straightaway the Genie's chains and lamp disappeared. The Genie smiled at his friend. "No matter what anybody says, you'll always be a prince to me!" he said.

"That's right," agreed the Sultan. "You've certainly proved your worth to me, too. What we need is a new law. From this day the Princess shall marry whomever she chooses."

"I wish to marry *Aladdin*," cried Jasmine in delight.

And that's exactly what she did.